Travelling with the Bedouin Women of Hawd

Somali Women Writers
Mama East African Women's group
Hooyada Africada Bari

Edited by
Amina Souleiman
Mandy Sutter

Illustrated by
Mary Sewell

MAMA East African Women's Group
2007

Published in 2007 by Somali Women Writers, MAMA East African Women's Group, MAMA Training and Resource Centre, Spital House, 91 Spital Hill, Sheffield S4 7LD, United Kingdom
Tel: +44 114 2752955 Fax: + 44 114 2757503
website:mamalink.org

Text: Somali Women Writers, MAMA East African Women's Group

Cover Image: Mary Sewell, freelance artist

Illustrations: Mary Sewell

Editing: Amina Souleiman
                  Mandy Sutter, freelance writer

Typesetting: Sheaf Graphics

Printing: Sheaf Graphics

ISBN: 978-0-9531101-4-8

This publication was supported by MAMA East African Women's Group and Arts Council Yorkshire Arts

Yorkshire Arts

Working Together
Conference 2006

Working Together
Mama link

Acknowledgements

The Somali Women Writers wish to thank the following people:

MAMA East African Women's Group, Sheffield, United Kingdom for supporting and helping to develop the stories and publish the book

The Bedoiun Women of Hawd for inviting us to their original, unspoilt and undiscovered world and for sharing their stories with us

Mandy Sutter for her understanding in shaping and expanding the stories organically, while preserving their spirit

Amina Souleiman for the initial interviewing and collecting the stories, for travelling to Hargeisa and Hawd to involve more women and for assiduously checking details and supplying the resources to perfect the stories

Jerry Simon for proof reading the stories

Laura Bell of Sheffield Libraries, Sheffield City Council for her support and willingness to help out and to work with the group to develop further projects

Delegates from the Working Together Conference 2006 in Hargeisa, Somaliland at Mamalink.org for their feedback

Abdullahi Abukar of Afgarad.com for helping to promote the book and other books published by MAMA

Mohammed Sheikh Hassan of Scansom publishers for helping to promote the book and other books published by MAMA

Mamalink of Hargeisa, Somaliland for their joint work and partnership

M Sewell

Introduction

'Travelling with the Bedouin women of Hawd' is a simple but we hope powerful attempt to convey a real way of life through a fictional story. Through it, we hope to engage, empower and give a specific group of women the opportunity to share their way of life with the rest of the world.

In the desert, the voices of the Bedouin women used to travel miles. Their steps followed.

But in the UK, where they are travelling on double decker busses to the city market, instead of walking with camels to collect grass, they travel amongst a people who talk in very low voices, almost whispering.

Their habit of talking loudly draws others' disapproval. People stare at them and embarrassment shuts them up.

If people were to listen, they would hear a lot.

Not about lions, snakes and mosquitoes, maybe. But they would hear discussions about whether it's best to cross the road when the little man is red or green. And why should it be a man anyway?

And if people were to walk with the women through the narrow streets of their new cities, they would see them looking up to the moon and the stars that used to guide them in the night and the sun that gave them warmth and strength, and wondering whether this is the same moon, the same stars, the same sun. Are these celestial bodies the same ones? If so, how

did they follow the women all the way to the UK? People would hear each woman's different answer.

But the women's tradition of oral storytelling, does not work so well in this new country. The only way they can keep telling their story is to find someone else to help them write it. This feels very odd to them. When someone reads Habiba's story back to her, she shakes her head and describes the result as a dish that lacks spices or any of the flavour that would give someone the desire to want more.

'My story has lost all its accessories and aroma, its jewels!' she laughs.

But we hope our story does not suffer from those deficiencies. And even if it does, we hope it will help the women's voices to travel again, and help their steps stretch further to escape the civil wars, and the greed and carelessness that has ruined their old way of life.

Travelling with the Bedouin Women of Hawd

The rainy season is over and the grass is at its longest and driest. Six Bedouin women, *reer miyi*, are busy in their encampment, preparing for their annual expedition to collect *maadh*, a special kind of long grass that they use to weave the walls of their habitations, *aqal*. The Bedouins move their encampment three or four times a year, but just now they are in Daroor in the Hawd region

This expedition is a special one. One of the women's daughters is getting married and the *aqal* they are building will be for her and her new husband.

The expedition might take anything between two and twenty days, and they have to take all their food with them. They are drying camel meat, cutting themselves new hide shoes and, careful as taxidermists, skinning killed sheep to make skins for carrying water, *sibraar*. As well as the dried camel meat, they will take dates.

As they only have four camels between them, they have borrowed two extra ones to make the journey with them. They have made frames for all the camels' backs, to hang their load on, as well as protective coverings for the camels' backs, *heeryo*. They have also made their own rope for tying the grass into bundles. These preparations have taken nearly three months.

The women's ages range between twenty and sixty. Ijo is the oldest, and Shamis and Sureer are also mature women. All three are grandmothers as well as mothers with large families. Habiba and Qamar are mothers with younger families. Nimo is the youngest.

The women are all loosely related to each other. For example Ijo, who comes from the Hagar tribe, is married to Shamis's brother, who comes from the Galool tribe. It is Ijo's daughter, Khadija, who is getting married.

The night before they leave, they stay awake for the entire night. The day has been cool and breezy – perfect weather for a long walk. Some of the older members of the tribe stay awake with them, to keep them company. They all meet at Sureer's *ardaa*, the open space outside her house. They are very busy, doing last-minute preparations and loading up their camels. They sing as they work to keep their spirits up and help to make light of the fact that they must go without sleep.

Sureer, who is fair-skinned with delicate features and a wide gap between her two front teeth, *faantax*, harnesses her camel (*raray*, a specially tamed male camel) with its *hogaan*. Then she grabs him by the *hogaan* and walks him to the spot she wants to use for loading. She calls him *tu, tu, tu* and he lowers himself to the ground and sits there, chewing the cud, *mayrac*, and gazing haughtily at the proceedings. He looks particularly proud and aloof tonight – rather like Sureer herself – and she wonders if it's true that a person's animals eventually begin to resemble their owners.

The women, wanting to get into their stride before the sun rises, have decided to leave their encampment just before dawn. Their men folk, children and the older people who stayed awake with them, have gathered to see them off. A wrinkled old grandmother hobbles over to them.

'Stick together,' she says. 'Keep a lookout for lion's footprints and high trees you can climb if you're unlucky enough to meet one. And watch out for snakes when you are cutting the grass!'

A stooped, grey-haired grandfather recites from memory a few verses from the Qur'an.

And then they are ready to go.

Calling their goodbyes, they step out purposefully in a rough group into open land, gathering momentum for their long journey. Like models on the catwalk, with their long necks and tall, erect bearing, they hold their heads high. The conditions, as yesterday, are perfect for walking, clear and breezy.

Nimo, a dark, slim young woman, is leading the camels, *hogaamin*, who are roped together, *xidhiidhsan*, one behind the other in a long string that stretches out behind the group of women. As she goes, she works intermittently on making a string, *sooh*, with acacia fibres, walking and twisting, walking and twisting. She tensions the string with her teeth, and as it grows longer, loops it over her shoulder.

Nimo, in her twenties, is the only one of the six women who is still unmarried (*gashaanti*). Where mature Bedouin women like Sureer and Ijo wear long straight shift dresses, Nimo wears a voluminous white robe, *saddex qayd*.

The robe is made from a piece of white cotton the size of three double bed sheets joined end to end. To make the dress, Nimo and Khadija stood at either end of the piece of fabric, twisting it into a tight rope that coiled back on itself. Nimo twists all her three dresses up after she washes them and stores them that way until she wears them. When she and Khadija finally undid the fabric earlier this morning, it fell into a multitude of tiny pleats.

Khadija wound two strips of cloth snugly around Nimo's breasts and waist.

Then she began to fit the dress onto her friend.

Laying the excess material over Nimo's shoulder, she set to work to pin the pleated material around Nimo's waist, making a long, full skirt that stopped an inch or two above the ground.

Once the skirt was made, she created a loose, flowing bodice from the remaining fabric, pinning and tucking it firmly into place over one shoulder, Roman toga style. At Nimo's waist, she hung a long red yellow and black hand woven scarf (*boqor* – literally meaning 'monarch of the dress'), and on top of this, a hand woven cord with a tassel that bounces as Nimo walks, emphasising every single step of her long journey.

Nimo wasn't sure whether she should wear her jewellery on her desert quest. But she decided she would, and her upper arms are now circled with the two precious bracelets,

sindiyo, her uncle made out of pieces of tin can. Tasselled earrings drop from the earlobes that her grandmother pierced, when she was little, with an acacia thorn.

Her hair is plaited close to her head. Two long plaits run from the back of her head up over her crown then diverge at her forehead to frame her face. Where the plaits end, her hair, strong and wiry, bushes out.

As the women walk on, the sky begins to turn bright orange on the horizon in front of them. Shamis, a round-faced woman with darting eyes and the fairest skin of all the women, looks back to check the camels and sees her shadow and the shadows of the other women stretching out behind her, long and thin, like black signposts pointing back the way they have come. The shadows of the camels are joined together in a thick, swaying black band.

'Look, look,' she cries, 'the sun is coming up! We really are on our way!'

The realisation loosens her tongue.

'Your bottom looks so much smaller in the shadow than in real life!' she says to Habiba.

'You look skinny in your shadow,' she says to Sureer. 'Like a wooden spoon, *fandhaal*.'

Habiba is used to Shamis's banter, and usually joins in with it, but not this early in the day. She breaks away from the group and goes over to a nearby tree.

She snaps a twig from an acacia tree, *galool*, and peels it. She walks back to the others, chewing on the twig to break the wood down. Moisture oozes out onto her tongue and she spits it out into the dust. Habiba, who though still tall, is shorter and plumper than the others and enjoys her food, thinks it's not a bad taste: like a root vegetable with tougher fibres. She uses its white splayed ends to brush her teeth, *caday*. Then she looks around for something else to chew. She sees, on a nearby bush, the soft whitish-green thorns that the Bedouin eat like fruit, *cambuul*. She picks a couple. She gives one to Ijo and eats the other herself.

'This is good,' she says. 'The last time I had one of these was just before I got married, on the walk with my mother to my new husband's territory.'

Ijo, the tallest of all the women, looks down her nose. She has a red patterned headscarf wrapped round her head and over her mouth to protect her from the dust, and it makes her look very serious. She is all long thin nose and large eyes, which glitter in her dark gleaming skin. Because she covers her mouth, her eyes have to do twice as much work to convey her expressions, and they scold and preen and flash in turns. They rarely smile. Her dress is striped in red and black and she wears the two gold bangles she was given when she got married.

'And is that what you gave him, for your first meal together?' she says.

Habiba is used to Ijo's acid remarks, and laughs. So do the other women, all except Nimo, whose admiration for Ijo makes her immune to the older woman's bossiness and frequent put-downs.

'I wish I had!' says Habiba. 'But no, I had to cook the best meal I knew! It was really difficult. It was the evening after my wedding.'

The women's ears prick up, sensing the beginning of a story, and they draw a little closer to listen.

'Everyone went home to tend their families and animals,' says Habiba. 'Even my mother, who I have always relied on. Before they went, they came to wish me luck and tell me to look after my husband, *nin*, and animals, *xoolo*. They forgot to tell me to look after myself! It was many years before I realised I had to do that too.

Later that evening, after a whole night and a whole day of dancing and singing and being surrounded by people, I was suddenly alone in the *aqal*. Even my husband had gone to milk the camels.

I sat behind the partition, *doc*, on a stool on the sand floor next to the fireplace, which was made of three large rounded stones, and realised I had better get on with my new life. The first task was to cook a meal.

I began to sort the millet, *hadhuudh*, in the wicker bowl, *masaf*, picking out the larger flakes, stones and straws, and sifting it, *haadin*, blowing out the dust.

My mother had taught me everything she knew about cooking. She'd taught me tricks about being a good, clean and tidy cook – like how to polish my *fandhaal* with ghee, to give it a long life and a shine. She'd told me that a good meal took a lot of preparation and that I had to watch my back with my new husband's family.

'You'll be judged by what you cook and what you do!' she'd said.

I was ready for the challenge but I must admit I was very nervous. So nervous that I kept nearly dropping the *masaf*! I knew there was no one from my tribe around that I could talk to, or consult if I was unsure of something. My husband's people seemed nice but I couldn't trust them yet. After all, I'd only been married to them for one day and one night and I knew they were watching me – watching not only what I did, but the way I did it.

After I'd prepared the *hadhuudh*, I got up and put some wood, *xaabo*, in the fireplace, onto the warm ashes. Quickly, it caught alight. I then put the clay pot, *dheri* on the fire and poured water in to fill it half way up. While I waited for the water to boil, I cleaned the house on the other side of the partition, sweeping the sand floor with a straw broom, *mafiiq*, and sprinkling it with water to dampen it down. I polished the inside and outside of the wooden milk containers with ghee.

It was already beginning to feel strange not to have to do any work outside! But tradition is tradition and I knew that as a newly married girl, I was not expected to go out of the house for a week or so. My husband's family were tending the animals for me and I didn't even have to collect wood for the fire, because my mother-in-law had already brought it in. This seemed strange too, since normally no one would dream of keeping wood inside – it might encourage snakes.

But the water boiled, same as always! I rinsed the *hadhuudh* and put it in. I threw in a pinch of salt and put the lid on for my millet to cook. I was very tired and needed some sleep.

But the words 'Look after your husband!' were still ringing in my ears and I knew I had to wait until the millet was cooked (at least an hour) and my husband was fed. I sat next to the fire feeling its warmth and the cosiness of the *aqal*. It was windy outside, and everyone was returning from a long day's grazing. Through the grass walls of the *aqal*, I could hear people talking and calling to each other; could hear the different animal voices too: goats, sheep and camels.

It was the rainy season, *gu'*, a time of celebration and fertility. The animals had grazed very well and their udders swelled, *godladeed*, with milk. I heard the women trying to round up the herd, *isu du adhiga*, to milk, *lis*, them. I heard them shouting, *qaylinaya*, for the children to help. I knew exactly what was going on – it was important that the women got as much milk, *caano*, from the animals as possible before they let the animals go to feed their own lambs, *naylo*, and kids, *waxaro*. The women yelled at the children to keep the baby animals back in the field, *edeg*. But the *naylo* and *waxaro* saw their mothers and started to cry 'maa maa maa.' The sound was deafening. The female goats, *riyo*, and female sheep, *ido*, were trying to run towards the *edeg* where their babies were penned in, longing for them, *ololeen* – they hadn't seen them since dawn. The women were holding on tight, trying to milk them and stop them running away at the same time. The children, *caruurta*, were shouting to the animals.

'Stop, stop, *joogso, joogso*, go back in the field!'

They were also shouting to their mothers.

'I can't hold them back any more!'

There was a crescendo of shouting, bleating and baaing.

It was so familiar. The same struggle would be going on at home at this very moment. Listening to it all through the grass walls of the *aqal*, I felt very homesick.

I began to give myself a stern talking-to. 'Home,' I said, 'is here, where I am now.'

But there was another voice in my head that would not be silenced.

'No!' it said. 'Home is where I first came from: the land where my people are, my tribal territory. This is not my home – it is my husband's home!'

Then, because I was thinking about home, I began to worry about my mother and whether she was having a safe journey back. She would still be walking – she had a long, long way to go, through tall *qurac*, *galool* and *maraa* trees, down treacherous paths, past snakes, lions and hyenas.

I began to wonder how long it would be before I saw her again. Would I ever go back to see my friends and family, to stroll with them, to fetch water with them, to talk with them?

Then I began to worry about who would look after her, now I wasn't living at home any more. I always helped my mother, you see, and made sure she had some rest. From when I was a little girl, I would massage her feet when they were tired, by treading on them gently. Who would do that now? I would rub ghee into her hair and scalp every month, to keep it healthy. Who would do that now? I would clean her nails and cut them with a little knife, *madiil*. Who would do that now?

Then there were the things my mother did for me. I used to love it when she plaited my hair. But now, because I was married, I would never have my hair plaited again. From now on, my head would be covered, as a signal that I was spoken for, and that other men had better keep their distance!

Then I started thinking about my new home and marriage. The house I was sitting in was loaned to my husband and I for the wedding period, *aroos*, but soon I would have to build my own home. My mother had given me all the materials, *surad*, I would need – we had carried them to my husband's territory together. They were all still rolled up, and the day I was to unpack them, everyone would watch and comment.

But at last my imaginings began to take a more optimistic turn. I pictured the day I unpacked my bundle and imagined my husband's people nodding their heads in approval at the beauty and quality of my mother's efforts – all the things she had made – and nodding at me with new respect. I saw myself building the most beautiful house this community of people, *beel*, had ever seen. I imagined their eyes and mouths open in surprise. I saw them talking about me until I was very old, respecting me and not only me but my daughter, grand daughter and great grand daughter. I began to imagine the kind of things they would say about us…

I was startled by my mother-in-law entering the room, carrying a wooden pot *dhiil* of fresh goat's milk.

'What's that smell?' she cried. 'What's burning?'

I jumped guiltily. She was right. There was a dreadful smell: singed millet. I seized the pot from the fire with my bare hands. I winced as the hot clay burnt my palms.

'What's the matter with you?' snapped my mother-in-law.

'Nothing,' I said, just managing to put the pot down quickly instead of dropping it.

Inside, the millet had boiled completely dry. I replaced the lid immediately.

'It's alright,' I lied, 'it's only a bit dry round the edges!'

My mother-in-law gave me a look, but put the milk down and left the room. I looked into the pot again. The millet didn't look good. But I thought I could save some of it – enough, anyway – and I guessed that my husband wouldn't be able to tell the difference. I scooped the good millet out of the pot and mixed it with ghee and milk.

A little later, my husband came in and waited in the other side of the *aqal*. I took the dish through to him. I was using my mother-in-law's wooden bowls, *xeedho*, and her *fandhaal*, and was nervous in case I dropped them.

But everything went fine. In fact, my husband thought it was the best millet he had ever tasted in his life. What a foolish man! In fact, it was burnt and gritty – I tasted it later. But I was very relieved. Even though the first meal I cooked wasn't a great success, at least I didn't poison anybody.'

Habiba laughs as she comes to the end of her story. But Ijo gives her a knowing look, *dhoolo cadayn*, as if to say 'Are you sure?'

Habiba's talk of her mother and mother-in-law has made Nimo envious, and she drops her head a little, to watch her feet stirring up little puffs of desert dust. Her own mother died giving birth to her, and her father, as is the Somali custom, went back to her mother's family and demanded another wife. But her mother's sister was only sixteen at the time, and has always seemed more like a friend than a mother.

'When should I start preparing for my own wedding, Auntie?' Nimo asked, when she heard that Khadija was getting married. But Auntie looked anxious.

'We'll think about that next year, Nimo,' she said.

Now, every time Nimo remembers that this whole expedition is purely to help Khadija set up in her new *aqal*, she feels worried. She is sure that she and Auntie should have started thinking about and preparing for her own wedding long before now.

Still, feeling sorry for oneself never did any good. Nimo lifts her eyes resolutely to the horizon. She is lucky to have been invited on this expedition, and has made a vow to herself to look and listen, and learn everything she can. She is also lucky enough to be able to look forward to being Khadija's bridesmaid, *minxiisad*, at her wedding. She will help Khadija dress, and then decorate her hair with paint made from drying and crushing fragrant seeds. Another opportunity to watch and learn! She straightens her back, and strides out, determined not to be beaten by fate.

The women walk on. Listening to Habiba's story and the familiar rhythm of her voice has helped them into their stride. They take long, loping steps and breathe deeply, swinging their

long arms and ample hips. They keep their eyes on the horizon. The sun is getting higher in the sky and the shadows are shrinking under their feet. The air is getting hotter. A bird sings.

Nimo calls out and points up ahead, to a shimmer of movement on the horizon. 'Look! Someone's coming our way.'

In a few moments the women make out a group of people approaching them. As the two groups near each other, they both slow down, and the women see seven men, of varying ages. The men shout out a greeting.

'What's the news? *Maxaa sheegteen?*'

'Peace. *Nabad,*' the women reply.

The camels don't like going slowly. They also don't like being bunched up together in the line. They start pawing at the ground and grumbling. So although the other women stop, Nimo doesn't, but starts moving off again with the camels.

One of the men wears a white sheet from waist to knee, and a shirt. His belt, *kiishad,* is made of animal skin. Its little pockets fasten with press-studs and his curved dagger, *toori,* hangs down from it.

'Have you seen any lorries going to the city?' he asks the women.

'No,' says Sureer. 'Where have you come from?'

'From Hodoyo,' says the eldest man, not deigning to look at Sureer, but surveying the way ahead instead. His hair and beard are dyed red, and he is carrying a stick. He has hardly stopped in his stride and now begins to move off.

'Be the guest of God, *magan Allah,*' the men and women say, to each other.

Almost before the men are out of earshot, Ijo starts muttering.

'That old man! Does he really think a little bit of henna can disguise his age? He's got an ego the size of the desert!'

Habiba looks round in case the men heard. But they are striding off, and in any case they are probably uninterested.

'Well, what do you expect?' she says, 'he's from Hodoyo!'

Shamis is thoughtful.

'I wonder what they're going to do in the city?' she wonders. 'They didn't even have a sheep with them.'

'Break into the shops, I expect,' replies Habiba. 'And steal some cigarettes.'

'With an ego like that,' grumbles Ijo, 'that old man must have at least three wives. Maybe he's looking for a fourth!'

The women walk on. They are entering a huge open area known as Banaano (Great Plains) where they can see for miles across the gently undulating land and scrubby grass. In the North loom the shapes of distant hills.

Nimo is some way ahead now, with the camels. Seeing the men has reminded her of Geedi, the young man she met last season at the well.

The tribe had only just moved to Moholin, and it was only the second time she had been to the well. She approached, with her camel and wicker panniers, *haamo*, and saw to her dismay that the whole area around the well was thronging with a recent arrival of camel boys, *geeljire*.

She stood at a little distance, watching while they jostled for position. They were shouting and pushing one another. She sighed. It was good-humoured enough, but she knew it might be quite a time before all their camels were watered. She lowered her camel, unloaded the *haamo*, and sat down on a little hummock to wait. While she was waiting, she noticed that one boy in particular seemed to command respect from the others. As he approached the well with his camels, they all got out of the way and let him go first. She couldn't help noticing that he was very handsome.

And then a truly wonderful thing happened. She still smiled every time she thought about it. As the other boys cleared a space for him, he happened to look up and see her, sitting on her hummock with her camel and her empty *haamo*.

She looked away quickly, but he had already lifted his hand and was waving her over.

'Let this woman go first!' he cried. 'We will wait until she has taken all the water she needs to fill her *haamo*, and water her camel!'

As Nimo made her way to the well, she felt embarrassed and thrilled all at once.

She encountered Geedi again soon after that. There was a dance, and during the *dhaanto*, when the lines of young women and young men moved backwards and forwards opposite each other to the rhythmic beat of hand clapping, stamping and whooping, he was there, smiling at her. In the *botor*, they circled each other, and she laughed and caught his eye.

Now her mind keeps flitting onto him. As well as pleasure and hope, she feels anxious: is she making a mistake, in liking him? He is handsome and strong but will he make a good husband? She knows little about him. Then she thinks of his smile and the way the other camel boys made way for him, and decides she is not making a mistake, at all.

The women soon catch up with Nimo.

'Meeting those men has made me think about the first time I went to the city, when I was fifteen. Half a lifetime ago,' says Shamis. 'I'd never seen anywhere like it!'

Qamar smiles. As a younger woman, she has been to the city many times. In fact, she had been twice by the time she was fifteen and has never been particularly in awe of it. But it is different for the older ones.

Nimo's ears have pricked up. 'What took you there?' she asks.

'My mother,' says Shamis. 'She took me to live with my sister, who was pregnant with her first child. She'd left our tribe two years before to marry a city man, and I hadn't seen her since.'

Nimo nods and listens, hoping to learn something.

'We were jolting along in an open lorry,' Shamis goes on. 'Driving at night. As we came over the hill into the city, and I saw the hundreds and hundreds of twinkling lights ahead, I was amazed – and also horrified. There was only one place those lights could have come from. I held my breath and looked up into the sky. My heart was beating hard. But – thank goodness – the stars were all still up there!

'Don't be silly, Shamis,' said my mother. 'They're lights.'

What were lights? I had no idea.

As we got nearer, people started to get restless, picking up their bags and preparing to get off. I looked at everybody, wondering who they were and where they were going. I wondered where I was going, too. What sort of place did my sister live in? My mother had talked about a thing called a stone house, but I had no idea what that was. I fingered the rough sacking we were sitting on in the lorry and wondered where I would be sleeping, and what I would be sleeping on.

Perhaps we would eat spaghetti, *baasto*. I had heard about it, but again, I had no idea what it was.

The lorry stopped and we all got out. My mother and I walked past some buildings that looked like giant boxes. She said that these were the stone houses, *daar*, and that families lived inside them. I didn't think it could be very nice inside: dark and stuffy. And the houses were built so close together! I couldn't believe that people could live like that, with no space around them. But I saw that some of the houses had a glow inside and that people were going in and out, so it must have been true.

Then, outside one house, I saw my sister Basra, sitting on a stool, *gambadh*, talking to the woman next door, who was also sitting on her *gambadh*. I suddenly felt very shy. It wasn't just because I hadn't seen her for a long time. It was because she was living such a strange new life. I thought she must have changed a great deal. But when Basra saw me, she stood up and held out her arms. She was very pregnant! As I ran into her arms and felt the warmth of her hug, I realised that although some things had changed, she was still my sister and always would be.

That night, we did eat spaghetti! It looked like long white worms, all squirming together on the plate. I nearly screamed when I first saw it, but my sister made such a face of pleasure when she swallowed hers, I had to try it. It was delicious. We also ate a yellow thing that my sister called a banana. When my mother saw it she said,

'How on earth do men smoke that?'

'It isn't a cigarette,' said my sister. 'It's a fruit!'

I slept with my mother in the back room, on a bed raised right up off the floor. I was terrified that I would roll off it in the night and crack my head on the floor. I didn't get any sleep at all!

My mother stayed with me at my sister's for a month. She taught me how to shop at the market and how to wash the dishes. There was so much water! We used a foamy thing called soap, *omo*, to clean the dishes. It was much easier than polishing the dishes with a cloth. My mother showed me how to wash clothes, and clean the cement floors of my sister's house. She showed me how to iron clothes to make them nice and flat. She showed me how to cook and how to make the fire up out of charcoal.

I started to get used to it. I made friends with the girls in the next-door houses and found out how to dress smart in the city way. When I went to market, if there was any money left

over, I would buy myself shiny things to make myself more beautiful – bangles, rings and necklaces. I learnt how to apply kohl to my eyes, henna to my hands and rollers to my hair. I bought a beautiful pair of high-heeled shoes. The first time I wore them, I fell over about six times. People laughed at me – it was so embarrassing!'

'Ah', says Ijo, 'you were stumbling about the place like a hobbled camel, *seetaysan*?'

'Or a new born ostrich,' says Qamar.

'Are you sure the shoes weren't still tied together?' asks Habiba.

'Was that how you met your husband?' says Sureer. 'By falling down right in front of his feet?'

'So he had no choice but to stop, or trample you into the dust,' adds Ijo.

Shamis raises her hands to the sky. 'I wish it had been that romantic!'

The women all laugh.

Nimo waits, hoping to hear exactly how Shamis did meet her husband. But she does not find out: mid-day is approaching and the desert is getting so hot that Shamis does not have the energy to carry on talking.

Nimo herself is sweltering inside her huge white robe. She glances enviously at the older women's dresses, made from just one layer of fabric, not yards and yards.

'I am so hot!' she says.

Habiba smiles. 'Why don't you tear your dress in half? Then it will only be half as hot.'

Ijo overhears.

'What do you think you're doing, Habiba, encouraging that child into bad habits! She's not

24

so badly off. When I was young, we had to wear twice as much material as that. We could hardly walk across the village!'

Habiba winks at Nimo. 'If it was me, I would take it off altogether and walk naked. Why not? We are all women together, aren't we Ijo?'

Ijo narrows her eyes and doesn't reply.

Nimo walks on, her problem unsolved. But help is at hand. The day is becoming too hot to walk, and the older women begin to scan the horizon for an area of grass and a big shady tree, *hadhac*, to shelter under.

It isn't long before they spot a cluster of acacia trees and begin heading towards them. The trees' flat tops make an island of shade on the ground, with plenty of room for unloading the camels. The women need a lot of room for this. Used to big open spaces, they don't like to be cramped together.

They pass a massive termite hill, *dundumo*, on their way to the trees. It is the height of two men and the width of five. Nimo shudders.

'What's the matter with you, child?' says Ijo. 'Termites can't harm you! They don't carry disease.'

'I know,' says Nimo.

But she can't help remembering how one of her brothers once broke open a termite hill and exposed the queen, a great fat white thing that he threatened to throw at her.

Ijo is still talking. 'Imagine how big you must seem to a termite! He will be a lot more scared of you than you are of him.'

By the time they reach the trees, they are dying to sit down and eat. But first they have to lower the camels, unpack the animals' loads and tie their legs loosely together, *seeto*, so that

they have rope to wander but not too far. It's hard work and takes them about an hour.

But at last, the camels are grazing on the sparse grass and munching on the leaves of some nearby bushes. The women spread the camel's coverings, *heeryo*, on the ground next to each other and put their food – yoghurt, dates, dried meat, ghee and water – in the middle. Each woman has her own enamel cup to drink water out of, white with a blue rim. To eat the sharp runny yoghurt, they make the palms of their hands into bowls and slurp it up. They eat the other food – meat and dates – with their fingers.

Of all the women, Ijo is the fussiest eater. She tends not to eat very much yoghurt, or very many dates, but stick mainly to the meat. Her teeth, rarely seen, gleam in her dark, long boned face. After eating, she rubs the thin remains of the yoghurt carefully into her hands, taking care to cover every single bit of skin and nail, then dabbing the very last bit onto her elbows.

Nimo is impressed. Covertly, so as not to attract attention from the other women, she takes a bit of yoghurt and rubs it into her own hands. It feels smooth, and she imagines it doing her skin good instantly, making it supple and silky.

Shamis is still thinking about her sister. As she licks her fingers, she remembers the party her mother gave for her sister in the last few weeks of her pregnancy, *sitaad*. They had to make a lot of food for that party. There were a lot of people cooking and her mother took the opportunity to instruct Shamis in front of them. She remembers how bossy her mother had been, and how humiliating it was to be spoken to like that in front of all the other girls and women. She'd felt incompetent because they were cooking with vegetables she had never seen before, and didn't even know the name of.

'Give me the cabbage!' shouted her mother, and Shamis grabbed something at random.

'No, no, you're not listening to me,' said her mother. 'That's an onion!'

Her mother kept delivering little lectures, sitting back on her little stool as if it were a throne.

'Original Somali food is very plain,' she said loudly, so that everyone could hear. 'All we do is boil potatoes, onions, basal, cabbage, tomatoes and meat together.'

I know that, thought Shamis. But she didn't dare interrupt.

And it was good to learn how to make *maraq*, a soup of boiled meat, onion, garlic and tomato, even though her mother didn't actually do anything herself: just ordered Shamis around – and any other girl who was unlucky enough not to be doing anything at that moment.

'You can put anything you want into it,' she announced, ordering someone to cut the meat, *hilib*, 'as long as it's vegetable or meat.'

When she'd finished telling one of the other girls how to put the meat and vegetables on to boil, she told Shamis how to prepare the spices.

First there were coriander seeds, *geedo*. She supervised while Shamis took two palmfuls, *laba sacab*, and roasted them in a little pan over the fire, then put them into the mortar, *mooye*, and crushed them into powder with the pestle, *tip*, while they were still hot.

'You'll need to mash it harder than that, daughter!' she cried. 'Give it a bit more muscle!'

She grabbed some garlic cloves, *toon*, from the poor girl who was trying to peel them.

'What's taking you so long? Do you think you're milking a camel?'

She gave them to Shamis to crush in the mortar with the coriander seeds. Then she told her to throw in a pinch, *qandhiidho*, of salt, *milix*.

Only when all the hard work had been done and the meat had been boiled until it was soft and chewy, did her mother spring into action.

She elbowed everyone else out of the way and separated the meat from the watery soup, *maraq*, with a flourish. She put meat and soup into different dishes and sprinkled Shamis' carefully prepared spices over them with satisfaction.

'Take it through!' she commanded. 'Normally, daughter, we would serve the men first, but there aren't any here today.'

'Does she think I haven't got eyes in my head?' thought Shamis.

But the food preparation, thank goodness, was done.

Shamis followed the food into the back room and all the women crowded in after her.

One woman was drying Basra's hair. It had been rubbed with ghee that morning in preparation for being plaited. Another was decorating the back of Basra's hands with henna. A third woman was mixing *qasil* powder – made from leaves – with water for Basra's face mask, a treat that would make her skin feel clean and silky.

After they had eaten the food, one woman brought a drum in and began beating it. Everyone started clapping. Once they were all in time, the drum woman led the singing. She called the tune and everyone else joined in with the responses. Shamis was grateful that at last she could join in with something that didn't make her feel incompetent. She didn't know the words to all the songs, but she knew some of them.

After a while, the women stopped singing and took a break. They drank tea and coffee and ate popcorn made from millet sprinkled with chopped dates. Shamis thought this was great. She sat next to her sister, and began to let some of her sister's glory rub off on her. But then something strange happened.

The women began talking to Basra.

'Remember that time you threw rubbish onto my doorstep?' said one woman. 'Well, it's forgotten now.'

'Thank you, sister,' said Basra.

'I hope you've forgiven me, Basra,' said another woman, 'for that time I borrowed your mortar and broke it.'

'Yes of course,' said Basra. 'I forgave you a long time ago.'

Shamis was mystified.

'Why are they talking like this?' she whispered to the woman sitting next to her.

Before the woman could answer, Basra fished around in her purse and came out with some money. She handed it to one of the women.

'This is the money I owe you for those gold earrings I bought from you last year. Forgive me for taking this long.'

The woman took the money graciously. Basra addressed all the women.

'If there is anybody I'm forgetting, please tell me now! I don't want to die in debt!'

'Die?' thought Shamis. 'I don't want my sister to die!'

She had heard of it happening to other women in childbirth, but until now, hadn't imagined it might happen to her own, dearly beloved sister.

Shamis is brought suddenly back to the present, and the hot desert, and Ijo's voice. 'What's the matter with you, Shamis?' she is saying. 'Are you wishing you still had those high heels?'

Although she knows Ijo is joking, this time Shamis can't laugh. She puts her face in her hands.

'Have you got a headache?' asks Nimo.

'No,' sighs Shamis, 'I was thinking about my sister, and how frightened I was while she was having her first baby. I heard her scream, but they wouldn't let me go into the room and help her! It was dreadful.'

'My mother died that way,' says Nimo quietly.

The women fall suddenly quiet, not just out of respect for Nimo. All have lost female relatives to childbirth.

'I know, Nimo,' says Shamis. 'And I have no business to dwell on the past like this, especially when everything turned out fine, thanks be to Allah. The son my sister had has just got married.'

'I am glad,' says Nimo softly. 'I am glad you did not lose your sister.'

Qamar begins searching on the ground. She gathers five small stones, and brings them back to the circle of women.

The others nod and smile and move closer together, ready to begin the game.

'If you drop a stone, you have to pass the stones on,' announces Ijo before they start. 'It's also a fault if you move or touch any stone while you are picking up another.'

Habiba groans. 'I might have known you'd go for the harshest rules, Ijo. It's hardly a fault if you touch another stone!'

Ijo narrows her eyes. 'Afraid of being beaten, Habiba?'

'Certainly not!' says Habiba. 'We'll play by your rules, if that's what you want!'

The game, which they Bedouins call *jagi*, after the sound the stones make falling against each other, begins. Each player has to pick up all the stones one by one, while tossing and catching another and keeping all the caught stones in her hand. Then she has to throw all five stones in the air and catch them on the back of her hand, before starting again, picking up not just one stone this time, but two. As soon as she drops a stone, play passes to the next woman.

Habiba drops the stones all over the place, but Qamar and Ijo are very good players.

'You are cheating, Ijo!' says Habiba. 'I saw that stone move!'

'If it moved, it was not because I touched it,' says Ijo. 'Can you feel the famous Banaano breeze? That was the culprit!'

They play on until Qamar wins. The women clap and whoop.

'Ah, you should have gone by my rules, Ijo,' says Habiba. 'Then you might have won.'

'That's true,' says Ijo. 'But what about you? The rules have not yet been invented on this earth that would allow you to win.'

'Only if there were no rules, could Habiba win,' says Sureer.

'And then, what would be the value of winning?' asks Nimo.

'That depends on the prize!' says Sureer.

'Are we going to give Qamar a prize?' asks Nimo.

'Of course,' says Habiba. 'If the old man with the hennaed beard comes back, she can be the one to marry him!'

The women stay under the trees for several hours.

Ijo takes out a little bottle of perfumed oil and dabs it onto the back of her hair. Nimo makes a mental note.

'It's much cooler now,' says Qamar eventually, 'I think it's time we moved on.'

Ijo gets up slowly onto all fours then pushes herself up to standing. She puts her hands in the small of her back and stretches, pulling a face.

'I've been sitting too long,' she says.

She looks across at the camels. 'Feeding time's over, boys!'

The long arduous job of reloading the camels begins. It's difficult to persuade the camels to lower themselves – they have got into the mood of grazing and resent having to go back to work. Sureer's camel is particularly unco-operative, and keeps jumping back up.

'*Tu, tu, tu*' she calls, getting frustrated as she sees Ijo's camel behaving so much better.

'You are dead meat (*axan*)!' she threatens. Her words fall on deaf ears. Sureer has to wait until all the other camels are ready to go, when she can get some help from Nimo and Habiba.

As the women start to move off, Qamar looks around at the tree trunks for some hard sap, *xabag*, to chew after the meal. She spots some, standing like a string of beads on the tree bark. She passes it around the group and the women throw it into their mouths. The sap softens as they chew, and tastes good.

The women move on. The sun is glowing softly. The desert is very beautiful in the late afternoon: the temperature is balmy and the birds are starting to sing. The women's shadows have moved completely around and are now stretching out in front of them, leading the way. Habiba slows her pace slightly, looking around her with delight.

'Hurry up!' snaps Ijo. 'Don't forget our mission. We must make the most of this time of day – it's the best for walking.'

The women soon get back into their stride. They pass a group of meercats, *shuuqshuuq*, who stand stock still in the heat with their little heads poking up, alerted by the vibrations from the women's footsteps.

'It's alright!' calls Nimo. 'We aren't going to hurt you!'

'Aren't we?' says Habiba. 'They look just the right size for a tasty snack!'

The women walk on, their long regular steps eating up the miles. Late afternoon softens into early evening.

The darkness takes its time to gather. The landmarks ahead get more and more difficult to make out. A lone ostrich runs swiftly away from them, its long legs covering the rough ground faster than any vehicle could. Hoopoos cry, and the chirruping sound of cicadas begins, a sound that will swell and fade intermittently as the night wears on. The moon rises, a thin transparent disc.

The women will walk all night, taking advantage of the cool. Now, as the darkness becomes denser, they change the structure of the group. Instead of walking in a line at the front, they split into three pairs, spaced out alongside the camels, like bodyguards. It is harder to spot predators in the dark, and if lions are on the prowl, the camels, not the women, are in the most danger.

The area they are walking through now is not known for lions, but later they will be crossing lion country, *Libaaxley*. Each woman checks privately for her knife.

Of all the women, Ijo is perhaps the closest to her animals and she is glad of the opportunity to walk with her camel for a while. Walking in the dark and hearing the intermittent screeches of foxes and hyenas has made her anxious about the goats she has left behind. Two of them are heavily pregnant, which makes them slow on their feet, and she hopes they will not fall victim to some nocturnal predator while she is away. She hopes, too, that they are not missing her too much. Her husband and sons are there of course. But they may not be so patient when it comes to filing down the goats' hooves or settling them down for the night.

A sense of contentment steals over her, walking at the camel's side. Camels do not make foolish conversation, unlike certain men. She puts a hand to the camel's neck, caresses wrinkles similar to the ones she is beginning to feel on her own neck. Her camel's skin is warm to the touch, slightly leathery. She begins to sing to him, a crooning song that she makes up as she goes along, a song she is sure the camel recognizes and appreciates. She sings teasingly of the shrubs that camels most like to eat, warns of the ones that upset their stomachs. The camel plods patiently on, picking up his big pancake like feet and putting them down, over and over again.

All Ijo's earliest memories of life have to do with camels. Her earliest memory of travel is of going across the desert in a long line of camels. Her earliest memory of nourishment is of drinking camel milk, warm from the teat. As she grew older, she learnt how to milk the camels herself, and then to groom them, brushing their coats and massaging their joints, cleaning their teeth with an acacia stick. In some Bedouin tribes, it is the men who look after the camels; the women who tend the goats and sheep. But Ijo learnt to do them all.

'Hey, Ijo!' calls Habiba from further down the line. 'You are spoiling that camel! Sometimes I think you prefer his company to ours!'

Ijo is saved from replying by Nimo, who has spotted a light on the horizon.

'We're heading towards a camp,' she calls. 'Maybe it's another group of women.'

'Perhaps it's that old man with the big ego,' says Ijo. 'Maybe he never found his lorry!'

'Or maybe he's after Ijo,' says Shamis.

35

Ijo sniffs. 'Get on with you!' she says.

As they get near the camp and hear deep voices, the women realise that they have indeed stumbled upon another group of men. Groups like this are common in the autumn, after the rainy season. It's the best time for feeding camels up, and the men travel around, grazing their camels on different sorts of grass and vegetation, *xergays*. The animals' droppings fertilize the land, and seed the ground with plants from different areas. The women approach the camp.

'What's this?' yells a man, as he sees them. 'We are being invaded by witches!'

Ijo draws herself up to her full height. She thinks quickly.

'You must have known you would never get away with it!' she booms, holding her knife above her head and bringing an extra glint into her eyes, an extra degree of sharpness to her nose.

'Remember the time you stole that young woman's shoes when she was fast asleep under the acacia tree? Well, that young woman was me! And I'm coming to get my revenge.'

One of the other men laughs and steps forward to greet the women. 'What's the news?' *Maxaa sheegteen?*'

'Good news. *War san*,' say Ijo and Sureer, stopping to talk for a few moments while the other women nod to the men but move slowly on. It's the way of the Bedouins not to stop unless they have to. If individuals fall behind for whatever reason, it's up to them to catch up.

'Which tribe do you belong to? *Qolomaa tihiin?*' asks the man.

'Reer Hagar,' says Sureer.

'What are you women doing walking around in *Libaaxley* at this time of night?' asks the first man, in a patronizing voice.

'We are going to Marsin for *maadh*,' says Ijo, as if she is talking to someone very stupid.

'We will give you milk and fire,' says the man, imperiously.

Ijo nods, as if this isn't of much account.

But she and Sureer accept the two branches, which have been held in the fire until they've caught light. As custom dictates, they do not say 'thank you,' *no nor*, but 'God bless you,' *Allah ha kaa abaal mariyo*. The men reply, 'Allah be with you,' *Amaana Allah*.

The other women have got well ahead, and Sureer and Ijo have to walk quickly to catch them up. While they walk, Sureer grumbles.

'You made fun of that poor man! But in the end he was really nice to us.'

Ijo shoves her burning stick into the sand to put it out.

'Nice?' she says. 'What did he think we needed burning sticks for – to set fire to ourselves?'

'For God's sake,' says Sureer, 'He was only trying to help! Be grateful for once!'

Sureer and Ijo catch up with the rest of the group and take up their positions at the back.

As the night has grown, so has the moon. It is full and casts a bluish light, showing the way through the darkness. Every time the women look at it they feel guided and filled with hope, as if a friend is walking with them and watching over them.

The women reach an area of grassland. They walk in a track in the middle of long grass and bushes.

'We are now in *Laan Mulaaxo*,' Ijo calls out to the rest of the group.

'The branch of Mulaaxo? What does that mean?' asks Habiba. 'Did this Mulaaxo, whoever she was, plant a tree here?'

Of all the women, Habiba annoys Ijo the most. She is always saying and doing exactly what she feels like. Ijo, on the other hand, values restraint – at least in certain matters.

'Do you know how this place got its name?' she says to the group, as if Habiba hadn't spoken.

Habiba and Shamis exchange glances.

'No, but I expect you are going to tell us,' says Habiba.

Ijo ignores her. 'Once,' she says, 'a woman named Mulaaxo was walking through this place with her companions, and a pride of lions ran towards them. Mulaaxo was very frightened but unlike her friends, she had great presence of mind and quickly climbed a tree. She told the others to do the same, but they were foolish women and could not recognise good advice when they heard it. They went the wrong way. But I stayed in the tree. I stayed there for a long time.'

'I?' says Shamis. 'Don't you mean Mulaaxo?'

'Did I say *I*?' asks Ijo. 'Forgive me. I meant to say Mulaaxo.'

She smiles as she speaks, to show she meant nothing of the sort.

'What happened to her friends?' asks Habiba.

'Oh, *they* were eaten alive,' says Ijo.

Nimo's mouth drops open in alarm, but the other women look at each other and roll their eyes.

'Anyway, I like this place,' says Ijo.

'Like it?' echoes Habiba, incredulously. 'Why?'

'Because it is the only place I know named after a woman.'

No-one can think of a reply to this. Ijo goes on talking.

'But we must prepare. Nimo you stay at the front, Qamar and Sureer go to the right. Habiba and Shamis: go to the left side. I shall stay at the back. If a lion is to attack us it will most likely attack from the back.'

'Or the sides!' says Habiba.

'I was coming to that,' says Ijo. 'We must keep a special eye on the right side as the vegetation is more dense there than on the left. Probably that's where the water site, *biyo mareen*, is.'

Sureer moves to the position ordered by Ijo. Ijo annoys her sometimes, with her bossy commands, but she doesn't want to fall out with her. And after all, someone has to take the lead, and she has no desire to do so herself. Ijo is still talking.

'I once had an uncle nicknamed Libaax Legde because he was good at fighting with lions. He would carry his knife in his right hand and a piece of sheeting in his left. He would wrap the sheeting around his left forearm and present it to the lion. While the lion was busy biting his arm, he would stab it in the stomach with the knife.'

'Oh,' says Shamis, rolling her eyes again. 'I'll use that technique tonight then, Ijo, when a hungry lion several times as big and heavy as me jumps out from the bushes. I'm sure that little bit of cloth wrapped around my left arm will really distract him!'

Ijo throws her extinguished stick at Shamis, who ducks just in time. All the women laugh.

'Perhaps you should,' says Ijo. 'But you'll have difficulty with it. After all, how can a foolish woman like you tell their left arm from their right?'

Laughter erupts again. It makes all the women relax somewhat.

Nevertheless, Ijo stays watchful. She keeps glancing into the thicket. The darkness obscures vision and the moon casts black shadows. She tries to remember everything she has ever heard about lions and how to spot them in the dark. Her father once told her that a lion looks white by moonlight. She thinks she can see something white moving alongside them, a few yards into the thicket. She tells herself off for being over-imaginative. But suddenly Shamis screams and points at the very same place.

'There, look there! I'm sure I saw one – a great big lioness, *gool*, stalking us through the grass. And look – the camels have all slowed down. They know. The camels know something!'

Nimo looks terrified. Sureer produces her knife.

'Don't worry,' she says. 'I'll take care of it!'

She dodges behind one of the camels. 'There's no sense in taking too much of a risk, though,' she adds. 'I'll let the camel be eaten first.'

Ijo glares at her. 'Get back into position, Sureer! Do you want us all to be eaten alive?'

She looks again at the spot. It's impossible to see anything clearly. But even if it is a lion, there's nothing to be gained by getting hysterical.

'Don't be silly, Shamis,' she says firmly. 'There's no lion. It's only the grass swaying in the night breeze. Look! It might look white, in the moonlight, but that doesn't make it a lion.'

Shamis stands her ground.

'No, I did see a lion!' she insists. She turns to Ijo. 'You don't know everything!'

But Ijo's reassurance has calmed everyone and they walk on gladly. Shamis takes her place again, muttering that the left hand side is just as dangerous as the right. She turns to Habiba.

'I feel sorry for the tribes living anywhere near this area,' she says, 'They must be continually in a state of nerves.'

Habiba pulls a face. 'Ijo's daughter will soon be living near here!' she whispers.

'Really?' says Shamis. 'Ijo,' she shouts, 'How can you let your precious daughter live with man-eating lions?'

Ijo, who comes from this area herself, has heard this question before, and it annoys her.

'I know more people bitten by snakes than attacked by lions,' she snaps.

Sureer laughs. 'Is that supposed to make us feel better, Ijo? When my old uncle was bitten by a cobra, *abeeso*, he nearly died.'

Nimo's eyes widen. 'What happened?' she breathes.

'Well,' says Sureer, 'we were walking on a track just like this with our animals and he was at the back. Suddenly he called out. 'I think I've trodden on something sharp!' My aunt, who was the sort of person who knew everything – a bit like Ijo – said, 'Better let me have a look.' But instead of sitting down on the grass to show her his foot, my uncle collapsed. My aunt knew then that this was snakebite, and poisonous. His ankle was swelling and he was losing consciousness.

'Help me, Sureer', said my aunt. 'Hold his head and talk to him while I get my box of herbs.'

She was a great healer, known and respected in many tribes for it. She would sometimes travel as far as Danood to heal the sick. Once, when two tribes went to war, she was away for six months tending people from both sides. She would heal people of all ages, from tiny babies to old men. She used all kinds of herbs. She used them fresh and she made them into infusions by boiling them up in water. As a child, the things she did used to frighten me. She would suck the bad blood out of painful areas on people's bodies with a piece of hollowed-out cow horn, *toobin*. And once, when I had a cold, she heated a metal spoke in the fire, then touched it to my skin in various places. It hurt so much I cried. But I got better.'

'What about your uncle?' says Nimo anxiously. 'Did he get better?'

But Sureer does not want to be rushed.

'Anyway,' she says. 'There I was with my uncle's head in my lap. I couldn't think what to say to him, so I sang a little song I knew, about looking after the baby goats. I don't know

whether he heard it or not because his head was lolling to one side, and he was moaning.

Soon my aunt was back with a bunch of crushed leaves. I held some of them under my uncle's nose while my aunt rubbed some more into his ankle. They smelt really strange. But I was proud to be able to help my uncle.

My father, who'd gone on walking with the rest of the group, noticed that we'd stayed behind. He stopped the walk and came back. When he heard what had happened, he sent some of the men off into the grassland to find the snake. They came back triumphantly, with a dead cobra.

'I don't know if that's the snake that bit him,' my aunt muttered, looking at the wound. 'But anyway, he's not going to walk very far. We'll need to carry him. Make those children get off that camel.'

The girls carried the children, and the camel carried my uncle, lying down flat on his back, until we stopped that night to make camp. Every so often along the way, my aunt gave him the fresh, bitter-tasting herbs to chew. He was still feverish, and vomiting, but my aunt knew that the herbs would make him better, so she was not worried.

But it took my uncle a long time to get better. And we had to stay in that place, snake camp, *Masley*, until he did. We made a special raised bed for him out of wood and my aunt prepared all his meals. She fed him a lot of camel meat and camel milk, to give him back his strength and build him up.'

'I wonder what it's like, to be bitten by a snake,' says Nimo.

'Before my uncle passed out,' says Sureer, 'the last memory he had was of goose pimples going right the way up his leg to his heart. When he came to, his foot was very swollen. He still has the scars. Pus came out of his foot for quite a long time after.'

'Ugh,' says Nimo.

'When my grandfather was bitten by a snake,' says Qamar, 'he died straight away. We weren't lucky enough to have someone like your aunt, Sureer.'

Shamis shudders. 'So we're not only watching out for lions, but snakes as well.'

'What signs should we look for, Ijo?' asks Nimo in a small voice. 'How can we tell if there are snakes around?'

'I was coming to that,' says Ijo, untying some leaves from around her waist.

'It's not as easy to spot a snake as it is to spot a lion, you know. But take these leaves and chew them. Snakes don't like the taste.'

Nimo frowns. 'But won't it be too late by then, Ijo?'

Ijo waves her hand dismissively. 'I've been chewing these leaves since I was five, and I've never been bitten by a snake.'

'Just do as the great healer tells you, Nimo,' says Shamis.

Sureer is still thinking about her uncle. 'And when he recovered,' she says, 'he was like a man ten years younger, thanks to my aunt!'

'Ten years younger?' said Ijo. 'So did he find himself a new wife ten years younger than your aunt, to match?'

The sound of a slap makes Nimo jump. It is Habiba, who has slapped her own arm.

'Look!' she says triumphantly, showing everyone the smeary remains of a mosquito.

'I've killed our deadliest foe, Ijo, just like that! Don't forget that more people die from mosquito bites than either snakes or lions! My grandmother got malaria, you know.'

Nimo is not sure she can bear to listen to another grisly story. At every turn, it seems, there is another enemy waiting to pounce. But the information might be valuable. She steels herself.

'What happened?' she asks, faintly.

'Well, grandmother was ill for a very long time,' says Habiba. 'And the illness was dramatic. One minute sweat poured off her, the next she was shivering, and we had to heap blankets onto her. She slept and slept, then woke up with terrible headaches. I used to massage her head, and it helped a little. She didn't eat a thing for months! Imagine that! She grew so thin. All she could do was drink the tea that my mother brewed for her. Everything else made her vomit. What a sickness that was. And all from one little mosquito bite!'

'How terrible,' says Nimo. 'When did she start to get better?'

'Oh, she didn't get better,' says Habiba. 'She died.'

Nimo clasps her arms around herself for comfort. She feels a little raised bump on her right arm. She gasps, and twists her arm round to look at the place.

'What does a mosquito bite look like, Habiba?' she breathes.

Habiba runs her fingers lightly over Nimo's arm and laughs.

'Don't be silly, child!' she says. 'That's only a spot!'

The women walk on. On the horizon, there appears the faintest glimmer of light. Habiba's feet are aching.

'Are we going to stop soon?' she asks. 'I'm hungry!'

'How can you be hungry,' says Qamar, 'when there are lions and snakes around?'

'Oh let them eat me!' says Habiba. 'At this rate, there won't be much meat on my bones.'

'We've got a good few miles, *geedi*, to go before morning,' says Ijo.

Then, because she is getting hungry herself, she relents. 'We can eat some dates and drink some milk while we walk,' she says.

'When we stop,' says Shamis, 'I'm going to make myself one of my famous breakfasts – kidneys with onions fried in olive oil with fresh pancakes, *anjeero*, and lots of spices. Cinnamon tea too, to calm my nerves after the trauma of the lions and snakes.'

'Are you trying to torture me?' says Habiba.

'That's typical of you, Shamis,' says Ijo, 'Just looking out for yourself.'

'Well, I might make enough for one other person,' says Shamis. 'The person who has been nicest to me on this journey.'

'Who's that?' says Habiba hopefully.

'Well, it's not Ijo,' says Shamis.

Ijo looks towards the horizon and sees the faintest glimmer of light.

'Ah,' she says. 'It's nearly dawn.' She frowns. 'And I haven't done my morning prayers yet.'

What on earth is Ijo doing, thinks Shamis – testing our bravery? 'I'd rather wait till I'm a bit further away from *Laan Mulaaxo*, Ijo,' she says. 'Even if it is named after a woman!'

Ijo looks annoyed, especially when the other women nod in agreement with Shamis.

'Well, I'm going to do mine,' she announces. 'Even if I have to do them alone.'

'That will be a rare thing,' Shamis says quietly to Habiba. 'Ijo doing something on her own! How will she manage it? There will be no-one to boss around!'

But Sureer nods. She knows the other women won't stop, but she doesn't mind. She certainly doesn't want to leave Ijo on her own in lion territory.

'You're right, Ijo,' she says. 'Let's do it now.'

Ijo and Sureer take their prayer mats from their camels and spread them out next to each other on the ground, both pointing towards Mecca. Normally, before the women pray, they wash their hands, faces, arms and feet three times in water. But here, they can only wash their hands in dust. They stand tall at the end of their mats and begin their prayers with the *Bisim*: 'In the name of Allah, who is most gracious, most merciful.'

The other women carry on walking slowly.

Shamis looks thoughtful. 'I feel sorry for Sureer,' she says. 'Always having to fit in with Ijo! I'm sure Sureer is terrified of lions. How will she be able to concentrate on her prayers if she is looking over her shoulder the whole time?'

Qamar laughed. 'Yes, but what can she do? I think she's quite fond of her. I suppose she's more used to her than the rest of us. Ijo has probably been bossing her around ever since she was a little girl.'

'No she hasn't!' said Shamis. 'It hasn't always been that way! Don't you know the story of how Ijo came to our tribe?'

All the women's ears prick up, especially Nimo's.

'What story's that?' says Habiba.

'Well,' says Shamis. 'One year Ijo's tribe, the Hagar, brought their animals onto our tribal land to share our water. It was a terrible time – the dams, *balis*, had all dried up. We'd put a restriction on what they could have – after all, we had to look after our own people. But they came back for more, bringing all their camels with them. I was only small, but I remember how we all gathered around the well, *ceel*. We could hear the *hugun* of them coming in the distance: the sound of dozens of people and hundreds of camels walking, the people talking and singing and the camels burning for water, *ollol*.

When they arrived, all our men stood around the well to stop them getting at it. But one of their younger men broke through with his camel and headed straight for the water. My brother Maraa stood up to them. He was so brave! He took up a stick and hit out at the camel, trying to beat it out of the way. Then everyone started shouting. There was a great confusion: their camels struggling to drink from the troughs around the well; their camel drivers scooping water out of our well with their animal skin bags; the men of our tribe bellowing at them to stop and trying to beat back the camels. The next thing, there was a gunshot! People ran everywhere. I heard my mother screaming, then saw her kneel down in the middle of the crowd, sobbing. I saw the young men of Ijo's tribe run away, leaving their camels behind, and I knew something terrible had happened. Sure enough, there was my brother, our brave young tribal chief, lying dead on the ground, with our mother howling and pounding her fists on the earth.

Our family were all devastated. The rest of us tried to comfort her, but our hearts were broken too. However, we had to get on with his funeral. A few hours later, as we were starting to bury him, three men from the Qudhac tribe arrived. They'd heard what had happened from the young men of the Hagar tribe and had come to arbitrate, to help us settle our differences. First they offered their condolences and helped us with our burial. Then they went to talk to my father and some of the other elders. That was the first of several meetings between the elders of the Hagar tribe and our tribe. I don't know what they talked about, but our tribe returned all the camels the Hagar tribe had left behind and two seasons later, a hundred camels, *kadin*, arrived – plus Ijo. Ijo was married to my next oldest brother, Qansax.'

Nimo's eyes are wide. 'You must hate Ijo after what happened to your brother!'

Shamis shrugs. 'I did hate her at first. And so did my mother. But she gave birth to seven strong, healthy sons. So she did her job well.'

'And it must have been very hard for Ijo!' says Nimo.

'Now I know why she keeps her head covered all the time,' says Habiba. 'It's to hide all the lumps and bumps inflicted by your brother!'

'My brother is a perfect gentleman!' says Shamis. 'And don't forget I'm telling you this in complete confidence. Don't you dare tell her I told you.'

A voice calls from behind. 'Time to stop for breakfast!'

Shamis jumps, recognising Ijo's voice. She and Sureer are catching up.

Shamis hopes she didn't overhear.

She nods fervently. 'Yes, yes, Ijo! You're right as usual!'

Ijo looks at her suspiciously. 'What's this – agreeing with me? You're not yourself today, Shamis. What has the morning done to you?'

'I can't wait for that cinammon tea, Shamis,' says Habiba quickly.

'And the fresh *anjeero*, pancakes!' says Nimo.

'And what about the kidneys with onions?' joins in Qamar.

It is time for breakfast. This will only be a short break, so although the women let their camels kneel down and rest, they do not unload them. The women sit down and bring out small quantities of dried meat and dates to nibble. Despite Shamis' dreams of tea, they will not go to the trouble of lighting a fire until they make a longer stop.

Qamar eats a particularly tasty piece of meat. 'Mm,' she says. 'This would taste even better with some flatbread, *sabaayad*.'

'*Sabaayad?*' says Nimo. 'What's that? How do you make it?'

Qamar is pleased to be asked for her advice. 'You make it from flour,' she says.

The other women settle back to listen. Even though every single one of them knows very well how to make *sabaayad*, they are glad of something to pass the time. And hearing how another woman describes things is always interesting: there may be an opportunity to correct her.

'You mix the flour with water and a little bit of salt,' Qamar explains. 'Until it becomes a smooth, soft dough. Then you stretch it out and fold it in half. You go on stretching it and folding it and stretching it and folding it until you get a nice square shape. Then you heat up a circular flat pan called a *dawe* and put the *sabaayad* in and cook it, flipping it over and over until it's light brown.'

Qamar holds her thumb and forefinger about half an inch apart. 'It's about as thick as this. When it's done, you take it out of the pan to serve it. You put the meat and ghee in the middle and roll it up.'

'That sounds delicious,' says Nimo. 'I wish we had some here!'

Habiba groans. 'Your description is too good!'

'I once met a woman from the South,' says Sureer. 'She said they don't eat as much meat and anjeero as we do. Instead, they eat a lot of vegetables.'

Ijo clicks her tongue. 'Do you believe everything you're told, Sureer?'

'Vegetables?' says Habiba. 'You mean onions and tomatoes? And garlic?'

'Not just those,' says Sureer.

'What do you mean, not just those?' says Habiba. 'What other vegetables are there?'

'She showed me an orange thing called 'carrot',' says Sureer.

'Orange?' says Nimo. 'Like a tomato?'

'No,' says Sureer, enjoying herself. 'Much harder than a tomato. It grows in the ground like an onion.'

The women look at each other disbelievingly.

'And some dark green leaves, called 'spinach.''

'How can people just eat leaves, like animals?' scoffs Ijo. 'I always knew those Southerners were poor.'

'Yes,' says Habiba, agreeing with Ijo for once. 'They sound like those good-for-nothing city men who sit around all day doing nothing, chewing qat.'

'It's worse than that,' says Sureer.

'Worse?' says Habiba. 'What on earth could be worse?'

'The woman from the South told me that there are some people who only eat vegetables and don't eat any meat at all! They are called vegetarians.'

The women throw their hands up in disbelief.

'Even I don't believe that!' says Habiba, and everyone laughs.

Ijo finishes eating her breakfast and stands up.

'Come on,' she says, 'time to move on while the air is still cool.'

Shamis groans. 'Already? I haven't even taken my shoes off yet!'

Ijo looks unimpressed. 'We will be stopping again before noon.'

'She's right,' says Sureer. 'Let's move. I don't think we've far to go now.'

The women clear up their belongings.

They move on. They are walking south-east, so the sun goes on climbing up the sky in front of them. They are well out of *Libaaxley* now. Three vultures fly purposefully overhead in the direction the women have just come. Ijo looks up. The birds will most likely be making their way to pick over the bones of a fresh carcass. Perhaps it was indeed a lion that they saw last night.

They pass some wild plum trees, *madheedh*. Qamar goes up to one of the trees and picks a *madheedh* from it. She wipes the dust off it with her hand.

'Is this the kind of fruit a vegetarian would eat?' she asks Sureer.

'Ah!' says Shamis, 'you have become a convert!'

Qamar smiles. 'I had been meaning to tell you.'

'What happened to that sheep that disappeared from your field last week, then?' says Shamis.

'The old man in our house ate it, not me!' says Qamar.

'I suppose you're going to tell us that he cooked it, too?' says Sureer.

'No, but I did cook it with carrots and spinach!' says Qamar.

'You mean you left out the spaghetti and banana?' says Habiba.

Nimo cuts across their joking. 'I can see grass!'

The women look to where she is pointing. Just above the line of the horizon is a yellow haze. They nod and murmur appreciatively.

'You'll be able to take your shoes off soon, Shamis,' says Sureer.

The women quicken their pace.

As they draw near to the grass, they see it covers a big area, stretching South, East and West.

'That grass looks very good,' says Habiba, 'long and strong. Good enough to build a thousand houses!'

'From this distance,' says Ijo dismissively, 'it's hard to tell.'

But as they get closer, close enough to see the grass waving slightly in the breeze, the women can tell that Habiba was right: the grass is good. The ground gets slightly harder as they near the grass. The sun is high in the sky now.

'There's a shady spot,' says Habiba, pointing to where several trees are growing together.

As they walk into the shade, Nimo makes an announcement.

'I've finished my string!'

She takes the loop off her shoulder. 'I'll use it to tie up my bundle of grass.'

The women walk into the shade. Habiba sits down immediately.

'Ah! Wonderful,' she sighs. 'Now, what can I have to eat?'

'What do you think you're doing?' says Ijo. 'You lazy woman! You must never sit down until you have unloaded your camel! Get up immediately.'

'But I'm so weary, Ijo!' Habiba replies, her eyes dancing with merriment. 'Surely the needs of people are more important than the needs of camels?'

Ijo's mouth sets. But Habiba is already getting to her feet, groaning and winking at Nimo.

'It's alright Ijo,' she says. 'I wouldn't dare to sit down before *you*.'

Ijo feels suspicious of this remark but decides not to reply. She turns, with dignity, and begins unloading her camel. What is she to do with this wayward young woman? But already some other piece of nonsense is happening. Young Nimo is rushing into the grass, brandishing her knife. 'Let me cut some grass!' she cries, glancing at Ijo to make sure she is watching.

Of course, she is doing it all wrong.

'No, no, no!' says Ijo. 'You don't use a knife to cut grass, you silly girl! And you don't bend down like that! You will injure yourself!'

Seeing Nimo's face fall, Sureer leaves her camel and goes over to her. 'Always start cutting from the edge of the grass,' she says, bending down gracefully, planting her feet wide and keeping her back straight.

'And this is the posture you should adopt. You'll be working for many hours, so it's important to take care of your back.'

She motions to Nimo to put her knife away.

'And you never cut grass with a knife!'

Sureer takes a handful of grass and pulls it. It comes up easily. Then she shows Nimo how to take a few leaves of grass and use them to tie the bundle up.

'When I first learnt how to collect grass…' she begins.

But Ijo interrupts her.

'Sureer, we want to get these camels unloaded before the next rainy season!'

Nimo looks gratefully at Sureer as they begin the long business of unloading their animals and setting them to graze.

By the time the women have finished, it is too hot to begin cutting the grass.

But it is worth lighting a fire, since they will be spending the night here. The

thought of cinnamon tea makes them all smile.

Fire is made by rubbing one stick inside another hollowed out one. Ijo gives this job to Nimo. Even though the sticks come from the *madag* tree, which should make the task quicker, it takes Nimo a long time because she has never done it before. The rest of the women decide they can't wait any longer, and begin nibbling at the dried meat.

'Hurry up, Nimo!' says Qamar.

'Yes, we are very thirsty!' chides Shamis.

'We'll never burn down Ijo's tribal territory at this rate!' says Habiba, giggling.

Nimo's eyes widen. Ijo glares, which makes Habiba laugh even more. Nimo feels annoyed with Habiba for being so rude to Ijo. But she admires her too. She longs for the day when she can feel that confident and grown up and stand up to women like Ijo without seeming to care what they think.

When the hole finally starts smoking, Nimo puts dried grass into it. She keeps rubbing the stick until the grass catches alight. All the women cheer as she piles more grass and sticks onto the little fire. Sureer fetches a tin kettle and fills it from her waterskin, *sibraar*. She has already built a frame of three stones around Nimo's fire and now she puts the kettle on it.

Soon the women are sipping the hot tea from their enamel mugs, and sighing with pleasure.

They rest for several hours and only when the main heat has gone out of the sky do they begin the task of cutting the grass, fanning out across the territory, cutting into its centre.

Sureer works as near Nimo as she can, keeping an eye on her.

So, when Nimo gives a little shriek and calls out, 'I've found a baby gazelle! In the bushes!' it doesn't take Sureer long to run across and grip the gazelle, which has become tangled in grass, by its hind legs.

Habiba and Shamis rush across, with Ijo and Qamar close behind, and before Nimo has time to say anything, Habiba has slit the gazelle's throat open with her knife.

'Oh no!' cries Nimo, upset. 'I didn't mean that we should kill it!'

She is full of emotion as she watches Sureer begin to skin the animal carefully and expertly, peeling the skin from the body with all the care of someone taking off a beautiful dress.

She knows that when Sureer has skinned the gazelle, she will tie it carefully, knotting its legs so that the cut up meat can be put back in. Then she will dig a hole in the sand, bury the skin, and move the fire to cover it. She will leave it there all night, and in the morning, when the women dig the gazelle back up, the meat will be the most tender, delicious thing you could ever taste.

And yet, the animal that has died was only a baby. Nimo feels confused.

She realises that Ijo is talking.

'Who found this animal?' asks Ijo.

'It was Nimo,' says Sureer, looking up from where she is working on the animal.

Ijo looks at Nimo and for once, Nimo does not see censure in her eyes, but something else, something softer.

'You have a good eye,' Ijo says, nodding. 'We will eat well.'

The other women smile and laugh and clap their hands to show their appreciation, and Nimo's confusion evaporates.

As she watches Sureer cut the meat up, Nimo thinks that having no mother might not be so bad after all. Not when she has all these other mothers to take care of her.

Epilogue

The Bedouin's way of life is under threat in modern day Somalia, where well over half the population is nomadic. For centuries, continual migration has been the pattern of life for most women like Ijo and her extended family. Small groups with portable dwellings move from one sparse area to another, giving the land time to replenish itself before moving back. But the last two decades have seen profound changes.

Ijo's daughter, Khadija, is unlikely to stay with the tribe after she is married. She and her husband will forsake a way of being they have come to see as old-fashioned, and will join the huge flocks of young Bedouins who migrate each year to the city. Khadija's husband, once a camel boy, will leave his elders to care for the tribe's animals. As the elders grow older and frailer they may not be up to the task.

This will be a real problem. Ijo is fit and healthy now, but this will not always be the case. And animals are central to the Bedouin way of life. Ijo is not unusual in her devotion to her camels: for Bedouins, animals (usually sheep, goats and camels) can constitute family as much as human beings. Camels in particular are highly valued for their desert-friendliness and their provision of milk, meat and transport for goods, as well as wool, hide, skin and bones to produce clothes, dwellings, carpets and blankets. They are a measure of wealth and status and are celebrated in proverbs and songs. In fact, Somalis have 46 different words to describe them.

Those same animals are also facing problems from 'Somali flowers' – the plague of brightly coloured plastic bags that are replacing the Bedouin's hand woven baskets and are beginning to decorate trees and bushes all over the country. Despite having been banned in some areas, the bags still litter the city and the desert, giving the animals that swallow them severe digestive problems and in some cases, choking them.

Plastic, although bringing some benefits, is also bringing problems to the Bedouin women.

When Ijo and the others build Khadija's grass walled *aqal*, they may decide to use polyethylene sheets instead of handwoven mats for the flooring. So far so good, but instead of the traditional wicker bowl, *masaf*, that Habiba used to sort her millet when she first got married, Khadija may make a plastic bowl out of a container formerly used to store chemicals. Without water in the right quantity, she will be unable to thoroughly wash out chemical traces. Neither can she smoke plastic to drive out germs, as Habiba would have done with her clay pot, *dheri*. The illnesses caused by these new problems will be unfamiliar to her and her family: she will not know how to deal with them.

During the long Civil War in Somalia, the Bedouins sheltered a great many refugees from the cities. However, city folks today tend to be unconcerned with the Bedouin's plight. As global warming accelerates and city people cut down the big acacia trees to make charcoal for exporting to the Middle East, the grass is drying out, and the patches of shelter are diminishing. The idea of no-man's land itself is beginning to vanish as land becomes more valuable and people buy it up and erect fences around their portion. The Bedouins wonder whether there will be anywhere left for women like Ijo and the others to lead their string of camels; anywhere left to graze their animals. They wonder whether there will be any high acacia trees left, to give shelter from the fierce desert sun, or to climb when they need to escape from predators, continuing the story of *Laan Mulaaxo*.

As Khadija and her husband, and perhaps Nimo and Geedi after them, turn their back on what is undoubtedly a hard life, there is a danger that the ancient wisdom, expertise and customs of their parents and grandparents will be forgotten. The Somali language itself is relatively new, and the Somali Bedouin culture is entirely oral, with wisdom, recipes, jokes and advice handed on through poetry and storytelling.

'Travelling with the Bedouin women', based on a series of interviews with former desert nomad women, has tried to capture the flavour of the Bedouin culture in writing. There are a great many stories still to be told. But we hope you have enjoyed this one.

This book is dedicated to the acacia trees of Hawd

The flat top trees that cool the air and cover the ground with expanses of shade

The flat top trees that give life and beauty to Banaano, the great plains of Hawd

The tall trees that feed and shelter animals and humans

The handsome trees that attract clouds and bring rain to their people

These trees are disappearing fast and they deserve to be saved.

Greedy business men are burning the acacia trees alive, to make quick money and to mass-produce charcoal so that the rich people of the Middle East may burn fragrances for their homes and smoke the Hashisha. The growing number of people moving to the cities is also contributing to the problem because they need charcoal for cooking.

The Bedouin Women of Hawd feel that this is a problem the world should know about.